# The Baby Boomers

## Teena Vaughn DAnnibale

*To the love of my life who supports me in every endeavor and always reminds me that I can do it.*
*I love you, Peter J*

# Contents


Title Page

Dedication

Introduction

What you need to know     2

The People     17

Names mean a lot     23

Chapter 1     34

Chapter 2     40

Chapter 3     45

Chapter 4     51

Chapter 5     57

Chapter 6     60

Chapter 7     67

Chapter 8     74

Chapter 9     84

Chapter 10     85

Chapter 11     92

Chapter 12     98

Chapter 13     102

# Introduction

Books by TeenaD begin a story.  You end the story.


It's a collaboration for those beginning to write who just need a little help with the process and/or editing AND for those seasoned writers who need a creative jolt to get the juices flowing again and have a little fun. I cannot wait to see how OUR story ends. Look for chances to share your ending on my You Tube channel Teena D.

Keep WRITING!!

Look for more Books by TeenaD that you can help write

the beginning or the end on Amazon in the near future.

FIND ME AT

www.youtube.com/watch?v=uOxpOPAjMvM

Blog

http://readteenad.wordpress.com

# What you need to know

# The ProLIFE

# Movement

ProLIFE is a government program that keeps people alive forever. Pro Life started as a movement to save babies from abortion but when Dr. Aaron Mathews, scientist and medical doctor, proved people could live forever with vaccines. Research money came pouring in after the 2020 pandemic, ProLIFE, with a capital LIFE, became a government program to assist people in living... forever. Lives of the already born became the priority.

# Religion

Religions like Christianity, Islam, Judaism were fading because of science. This opened endless avenues of research into healing disease. Without the powerful lobby groups influencing government in America and around the world laws became science-based and soon humanity was cured of all ills.

# <u>The Soul</u>

The question of a soul was also proven to be scientifically true.

The Native American belief that a baby's soul waits in the corner of the room when a mother is giving birth and enters the body with the baby's first breath helped in proving the soul did exist and is what made a person who they are, the body just being a vehicle. In the beginning, because of the wide-spread influence of the Christian belief that there is an unlimited number of souls and despite warnings from Mathews and others, medicine and science, supported by the government, proceeded with the Pro-LIFE movement with no plan in place for future pregnancies.

# Questions

1. What will happen if no one dies and all the souls are in use?
2. Where will the souls for new life, aka babies, come from?
3. What if someone *wants* to die?

4. Are souls connected to families?
5. Do they "live" outside of the body?

These questions, among other, were left unanswered. Over time, as souls were unavailable due to the ProLIFE movement's success in not allowing death of any kind, women got pregnant and would deliver dead babies because there were no souls for the new body. The soul was the life of the body and there were no souls left. Dead birth becomes what is expected when one becomes pregnant and there is little hope for a new generation. However, because Roe vs. Wade was overturned abortion is illegal despite women carrying a baby that will most certainly be dead at birth and contraception can only be had on the black market.Pregnancy is just a part of life and death. The only death people know are babies and extreme accidents when the Government Doctors declares the body unsalvageable. When this happenes the most joyous experience became possible. A LIVE BIRTH.

# The ProCHOICE Movement

Living forever began as a choice. The ProCHOICE (all caps) movement was an offshoot of the Pro-Choice movement, a group that felt it was a woman's right to decide to keep her baby or abort it was her own. Since there are no live births because all souls were in live bodies, the new ProCHOICE group changed their focus on death. They felt it was a person's choice to live forever or die. After a Supreme Court decision made it illegal for a person to decide to die based on similar arguments that overturned Roe v Wade, ProCHOICERS had to go underground to avoid prosecution by the government. The amount of government intervention necessary to stave off the COVID19 pandemic of 2020 stuck around when it came to healthcare. While this was great for life saving research like Dr. Mathews', it strangled many freedoms, trickling down like a crack in a windshield and spread into areas of people's lives no one could have predicted.

# The Baby Boomers

A group called the Baby Boomers was formed as an offshoot of ProCHOICE with a slightly more radical vision of the right to die. They helped people have "accidents" where the body was unsalvageable by government standards. Doctors then had to "declare the death" thus freeing the soul. This kind of assisted suicide had about the same split in support as abortion did years ago. Dr. Aaron Mathews became associated with this group so he could try to track where the soul goes after death. He was trying to prove souls are recycled among families. With this knowledge he hoped to overturn Bricker vs. PA thus freeing up souls for new life. He never dreamed his original research and findings would lead to such extremism and felt this proof would sway the government back to supporting new generations being born.

# Bricker vs. The State of Pennsylvania

The Right to Live law upheld by the Supreme Court forbade

suicide. It punished the living family members of a person who

committed suicide by taking away worldly possessions, careers, homes and status, and in cases of assisted suicide, imprison-ment. Norm Bricker sued Pennsylvania after his wife, Elaine, committed suicide to free up a soul so their daughter could have a baby. Bricker's attorneys argued that the soul belonged to the family and it was theirs to do with as they wished, a similar argument lawyers used with women's bodies and abortion. The government disputed the evidence that souls belonged to the living as well as the fact that souls were recycled in families and argued that the soul was now "up for grabs", so to speak, and was a detriment to society since no one could know what unsuspect-ing woman would give birth unwillingly to a live baby now that there was a soul available.

The court sided with Pennsylvania, changing lives and our society forever.

# The People

## "Old Souls"

Characters in the book who have been alive with the same soul long enough to remember pre-ProLIFE. Most are ProCHOICE but are afraid of the government or to speak up. The Baby Boomer movement is slowly winning this group over but the prospect of the horrific death necessary to release the body from being saved by the Government Doctors is unnerving and making it hard to change minds and convince people to commit suicide for the next generation to be born.

## "Saved Souls"

Characters in the book who were born because of a ProCHOICER's decision. They are related to the person whose soul they possess because Mathews is right, and souls are recycled within families. They are super intuitive because the decision to die was with intention and the soul is directed to the offspring of a relative by the person choosing to die. This is facilitated by a "Spiritualist" who is present at the suicide and birth.

## "New Souls"

Characters in the book who were born because someone died due to a real accident that rendered their body unsalvageable by Government Doctors thus releasing the soul to someone in their family who wasn't ready to receive it. Someone is pregnant, expecting a dead birth, and the baby lives. The mother probably doesn't even know the relative who died.

## "Free Spirits"

People who die due to accident and are unsalvageable but have no female heirs to inherit their spirit or male heirs with intention to procreate and are left to roam the other realm. They are often seen as beams of light. These people exist, they just have no body. How they handle this existence is varied. Free spirits are how Dr. Mathews discovered the soul exists.

## "Spiritualists"

A person who assists in a death and helps the soul into the human body at birth.

# Names mean a lot

**Dr. Aaron Mathews** - means miraculous gift. Unknown "soul origin" but appears to be an old soul. He is a scientist and doctor who saves humanity with a cure for death. He proves the spirit exists with help from Norm Bricker and Elaine, his wife.

**Dr. Mary Eir Mathews** - Maiden name, Eir, means goddess of healing, gift. Unknown soul origin but appears to be a new soul. OB/Gyn. Works with Axel Truman. Has known Norm and Elaine since they were all young.

**Norm Bricker** - means seeking truth, lives by a bridge (from old to new). We don't know much about his soul because it is before discoveries, but he appears to be an old soul. He gets arrested when Elaine gives her soul to her granddaughter, Jessie. He was a brilliant reporter, but all was taken away when he lost the lawsuit, Bricker vs. PA, because Elaine committed suicide. He is old friends with Aaron Mathews and wrote articles about his discoveries back in the day for the news.

**Elaine Beam Bricker** - means bright shining light, Native American family. We don't know much about her spirit, but she appears to be an old soul. She was born before discoveries. She married Norm when they were young and had Janine on the day her mom, Eelie, died. She is a women's rights activist.

**Eelie Beam -** means uplifted soul and she is Elaine's mom and Dusanka's daughter.

**Dusanka Beam**- means soul spirit - the spirit or essence of the person is believed to live on after their death. She is a free spirit (no body - a light dancer). She is Elaine's great grandmother and was a spiritualist and healer in her Native tribe. She can travel between realms.

**Janine Elaine Bricker** - means God is gracious. She is Norm and Elaine's daughter and a saved soul. She has Eelie Beams' soul. She goes insane because Aaron Mathews, father of her child, leaves her and is institutionalized. Her mom died to give a soul to Jessie, Janine and Aaron's daughter.

**Jessie Beam Bricker** - means gracious gift. She is Norm and Elaine's granddaughter. She is a saved soul and has Elaine's soul. Her father is Dr. Aaron Mathews. Her mother is Janine Bricker.

**Mylove Jessie Bricker** - a live baby! Her name means gift of love. She is Norm and Elaine's great granddaughter and a saved soul. She has her mom Jessie's soul. Janine Bricker (still alive in asylum) and Dr. Aaron Mathews are her grandparents and Norm Bricker is her great grandfather. Her father is Axel Truman.

**Axel Truman** - means peace, hope and faith. He is the husband of Jessie Bricker and is Mylove Jessie's dad. Spiritualist. Works with Dr. Mary Mathews in the "maternity ward".

# Chapter 1

*Jessie*

She just can't stop. She cries and cries and sometimes screams. She wishes she could be like other women and not care but she can't. She looks down at her growing belly wondering why she always clings to hope for so long and thinks, "Please let someone die."

The one bedroom they are allotted by the government is still and quiet this time of day allowing her the luxury of pretending she is alone. There is a beam of light peeking through the standard vertical blinds in her apartment, creme or grey were her choices. She chose grey. She looks back at the beam where particles of dust are dancing in the center, having their own little party. She vaguely remembers a story that her grandmother had called that kind of light a "beam from God". But she didn't know her grandmother or her parents for that matter so who knows.

She looks up and he's standing there. It's as if he can read her mind and he gently touches her hand, "It will be alright this time. I have a feeling."

She says nothing, but her eyes give it all away as she wipes a tear and continues to cut the vegetables. That is what he thought the last time. That is what he said the last time. The way he spoke so gently, touched her hand so knowingly, made it seem like he had talked to them, to the men her friend told her about. He made it seem like he finally understood how important this was to her and arranged for a soul since she had no one to leave her one. But he hadn't. She just knew. Last time it all fell apart just like it will all fall apart this time. Just like it does for everyone, every time.

He turns on the TV. The beam of light is now bent a little and sitting on top of his head, like a hat, no halo. Is that what her Grandmother would call it, a halo?  One of her most vivid memories or was it just a story someone had told her, was of the beams of light with souls dancing in them. She wasn't quite sure what was real anymore. It almost felt like she just knew these things, like they were a part of her soul but not her life, not THIS life anyway. Did she have a life before this one? She saw that on a TV show once. Her feelings get all confused inside of her nowadays making her believe she was there watching the beams with her mother. But that is impossible. They say it's the pregnancy, but she knows differently. She feels this way whether she is pregnant or not. Almost like her soul belonged to someone she knew.

The news blasts from the TV. Something about some new discovery. Souls and families? What? That's not what we were taught in SexEd, that's for sure. She smiles to herself. SexEd is nothing like the real world anyway. Everything is sugar coated, that's for sure!

She hears the bathroom door close and sighs, shaking her head at her own internal ramblings. A sharp whistle in the distance and it all begins; doors slamming; feet, so many feet: stomping, running, walking; muffled voices talking behind all of the doors, so many doors, so many accents: German, Spanish, Israeli, English; smells, smells that waft in through the seams of her door and make her want to vomit. It all makes her want to scream and run. But where would she go?

She looks at the vegetables.

The toilet flushes.

The TV is blaring.

The words are still muffled.

The feet are still walking.

The people, still talking.

The smells are still wafting.

The beam is still peeking.

The belly is still growing.

She wonders if it will ever go back to how it was.

When she looks up, the beam, the one from her Grand-mother's God, the one with the dancing spirits is gone.

She picks up the knife.


She heads to the bathroom.


He doesn't notice.


There is no hope.

# Chapter 2

*Norm Bricker*

Thank God the crying is over. There is nothing that can drown that out. Nothing that can wash that out of his subconscious or his conscious for that matter. He grabs a beer and sits down to try to meditate. A beam of light streaks onto his face, a free spirit. He thinks about how people used to call them lost souls and how badly he felt for them. Now, now he envies them.

This place is stifling. Smells, accents, noise and then the screaming from the women who will never be mothers. It's all too much, Soul crushing. As if his soul hasn't been crushed enough in this world without having to endure the screams when they lose them. Everyone can hear. Everyone knows why because it happens in every household. It has become a fact of life, or death, he guesses. Women, men, they all just move on. Sheep. But *this* one, she is always so pained by it. "Why does she always hold onto hope for so long? She must not have a mother to help her understand," he thinks out loud.

He tried to meditate again, the noise has died down a bit, more bearable. His beam has meandered over to the table and he watches the dust dancers. His wife loved the dust dancers. He watched the light and remembered how she would delight in the way Janine would giggle when the two women would sing for them. He loved to watch as Elaine and her mom sang and danced around the room with Janine, their movement swirling the dust dancers into a frenzy, creating a mosh pit ballet of sorts, all of the souls dancing together, the living and the dead.

He shakes his head violently and slugs down his whole beer, getting up for another, "No! Do not think about that, you dumbass. Hold it together."

But the daydream persists until the beam climbs the wall and exits through the ceiling and the darkness engulfs him and he is able to succumb to the only peace his soul will ever know, as temporary as it is, sleep.

He dreams.

His friend talked him into coming to this bar on Christmas Eve. "What kind of bar is open on Christmas Eve for God's sake," he says.

But it's packed. "Heathens," his friend comments with a punch in the arm and a wink as they enter the womb-like environment where sperm search for their perfect egg.

It's an incubator of sorts, everyone squirming, maneuvering for a good position to find the right one. The "one" that will allow a union, that will create a "forever" and provide security and a prolific life. "Two will become one" is how the church used to say it. And then one must add children to hold it all together like glue.

"The children are the key, the secret ingredient," Norm thinks.

There are all kinds of things that can go wrong between two people but when there are kids involved somehow people go above and beyond to hold it together, to hold the family together. It's just human nature.

Norm scans the room and thinks, "Same ole, same ole."

And then she turns. Elaine. His soul's mate.

# Chapter 3

*Elaine*

"How the hell did I let myself get talked into coming out to a bar on Christmas EVE!" she wonders aloud because no one can hear a blessed thing anyone says. The whole place reminds her of being at the bottom of a pond. The patrons are like those weeds that peek up from the murky bottom trying to reach the beams of light that scream down from the surface piercing the darkness. Everyone is trying to reach for the light whether surviving above or below the equator of water dividing the drowning from the living. "We all crave the soul dancers," she thinks.

Her mother Eeli and grandmother Dusanka made sure she practiced her Native American heritage. These women told her of the soul dancers when she was a child. Sitting at her grandmother's feet, looking up at her mother, she listened to the two most blessed people in her life; the two women who always told her truth and held her inside of their souls every day; the two women who loved her to the moon and back and as much as all the grains of sand in the ocean; they told her of the souls that show themselves to the living as dust-like creatures in beams of light above the water and as bubble-like creatures in the beams of light below the water.

These souls were waiting for bodies. "When a baby is born," her grandmother said with tears glistening in her eyes, "the soul waits in the room to enter its new body. They are our relatives and cannot wait to come join us again on Mother Earth. After hours of waiting and watching their relatives suffer to deliver their new body, the soul is ready. The mother will be ready to give her last push and the midwife and/or spiritualist will look up to see the soul and if the soul is ready, it is only then that she will tell the mother, 'Pushhhhh!' and she will watch as the head of the new child breaks out of the darkness and into the light. The new mother is screaming and in all the chaos the soul quietly slips into the baby's body with its first breath."

It was one of those memories that transports you to that exact moment no matter how long ago it actually happened. Elaine can feel her mom gently caressing her hand and the smell of her grandmother's hair. It smelled like water, even though water doesn't really smell like anything, that is what it smelled like. "Fresh," she guesses.

Fresh is NOT the word she would use to describe *this* joint, but it is what she would call Kevin who thought he was handsome from birth and who had sauntered his way over to her from across the room and was grabbing her ass. She was about to slap his grimy face when a guy stepped in and punched ole Kevin right in the nose! "Goddamn it, Norm. What the hell?" screamed Kevin, blood dripping between his fingers as he started to come at Norm.

Elaine backed away to the corner of the bar, thinking the bartender would protect her from these two lunatics, but he was busy flirting with a blonde girl with barely any clothes on and boobs bigger than her head.

"Time for you to leave before I give you more of the same," she heard Norm demand.

"Well, fuck you then, find your own ride home, asshole."

And with that Norm turns to Elaine and says, "I apologize for my friend's behavior. I am Norm Bricker and you have the most beautiful eyes I have ever seen."

"I am Elaine. And thank you, I think. I certainly could have handled that jerk myself. He has been that way since high school. He must have gotten you pretty good when you weren't looking, though," she said staring at his right eye.

Embarrassed Norm touches his blackened face, "Uh, he didn't touch me. I got this boxing at Attica Prison."

"You were in PRISON?" she says backing up toward the bar again, scoping out a safe way out of this corner.

"No, no, you don't understand. My college team was boxing the prison boxing team as an exhibition and…"

"Oh my, well, I have a feeling the other guy musta looked worse if tonight's performance is any indication."

Norm turns to face her, and she looks at him seriously for the first time and realizes this is the man she would marry.

# Chapter 4

*Elaine, Norm, and Janine*

It was the best day of their lives. A girl. The world outside of the hospital room was whirling with political tension and a huge Women's March. But in *this* room, in *this* moment there was only them. Her breath on Elaine's chest. Her tiny feet in Norm's huge hand. She sighs, the tiniest of sighs. Norm looks at Elaine and whispers, "Thank you."

The nursery was in a corner of the living room in their one-bedroom apartment. Elaine had put up bright yellow curtains with flowers and had painted the whole place lavender. Norm really didn't dig the lavender, but hell, they couldn't afford an apartment with two bedrooms and his wife, soon to be a first-time mom, had to make a nursery in the living room, so he didn't say a word. She never complained once and was" happy as a clam to just be with him." She said she didn't care what ocean she was in as long as they were clams together. When she said these things he would kiss her forehead and not just because he could barely reach her lips anymore because of her big belly but because he just couldn't love anything or anyone any more than he loved her...or so he thought until Janine was born.

Besides, the two of them never left the bedroom, they were like rabbits, so what did he care what color the living room was. "Who knew pregnant women were horney as hell," he chuckles to himself as he watches her singing while making sauce for dinner with her big belly knocking everything over in her purple kitchen with the yellow flowered curtains.

Despite their unbelievably happy life filled with love for one another and the fact that they felt like the luckiest people in the world, life lately was a mess. Elaine's mom, Eeli, had been sick for quite a while. Eeli was Elaine's spiritual guide. Norm was her true North, her rock here on earth, Eeli was who Elaine turned to for spiritual guidance. And it was killing her that there was a big chance that Eeli wouldn't be here for the birth of her child.

It didn't help matters that Norm was covering the political tension evolving from all of the research his friend Aaron had un-covered. Norm's job at the newspaper was relentless with the talk about the discovery of the key to longevity.

The Alzheimer's Research Association had unearthed new information during the post pandemic research burst about a virus that was infiltrating the Limbic system of the brain and was a direct cause of Alzheimer's. The virus is contracted in your youth and slowly destroys the memory as well as various other life ending problems. The new researcher, Dr. Aaron Mathews, is a hair's breadth away from the next best thing to the fountain of youth, a cure for all ills; in other words, unless you are hit by a train or kill yourself, you could live forever. It's a mind-bending concept and Norm has been covering all the new findings. He has an in with Aaron since they protested the war together as young men and let's face it Aaron has needed some honest publicity what with all the wackjobs protesting his research as "playing God".

It hasn't hurt Norm's career either. Covering breaking news front page stories for the last six months that are life changing for the whole world is every journalist's dream. But it couldn't have come at a worse time for he and Elaine, what with her being pregnant and her mother deathly ill. Norm worries every time he gets called out on assignment that she will lose the baby or his mother in law will die. It seems that less people are dying and less are being born to him. It's probably just a coincidence, his mind wandering into dark places because of all the stress. But it is an angle he wants to pursue after the baby is born.

"Elaine, you won't believe the day I had," he throws his backpack onto the kitchen table and searches the frig for dinner. "What the heck is wrong with this frig, it's warm again. Damn it if those right to lifers aren't picketing John's offices again. It seems they are switching from abortion to…" He stops dead in his tracks.

Elaine is sitting in the dark living room. He realizes the lavender walls look more eggplant in color and there is no music. If Elaine is around there is always music.

There is one beam of light streaming through the bright yellow curtains with flowers. Norm notices that it lands on her huge belly and stops there. She lifts her head and looks at him through tear-soaked hair, "She's gone and she's," pointing to her belly, "coming."

That was yesterday. But all Norm could see right now was his beautiful Elaine nursing their daughter. How did she know it was a girl, he wondered? Right now, his whole existence was about wonder. They named her Janine, Janine Eelie.

"'One soul gone another comes.' That's what Dusanka always said." She looks at her baby and cries.

# Chapter 5

*Mary Mathews*

The live birth that came in last night really was unbelievable. She was having a late dinner with a colleague after another of probably a million D and Cs, "We gotta clean 'em out, Mary," Sam would chuckle. "They won't ever quit hopin' and if one of 'em ever does have a live one we gotta have her in tip top shape.", and they got called to the ER STAT.

She ran down the back stairs, the one that smelled like

dead cats. They never get called to the ER. I mean why would they the way things are now and as the stairwell door opened so did the ER doors and in walked Norm Bricker holding a towel in his arms followed by a guy who looked like he got hit by a truck driven by a ghost. "Norm Bricker, what the hell happened to you?"

He just stood there and stared at her. Now Norm wasn't too talkative to start with since everything that happened with Elaine and his daughter going crazy and all, but it was an EMERGENCY room and she was a GYNECOLOGIST and he was a GUY. So what did he need her for? And then she heard it. A cry, a tiny cry, a whimper, and looked down and in Norm Bricker's arms was a baby. A live baby! Norm fuckin' Bricker was holding a live baby. The entire room was dead silent except for Sam complaining about having to run down four flights of stairs because the, "elevators were as broke as a whore in a town full of unics" and the quiet sobbing coming from the guy who looked like he got hit by a ghost truck. When she took a longer look at him she realized that was Axel, Axel Truman. Wasn't his wife pregnant! Where was

SHE?

Mary reached out and looked at Norm, who had tears running down his cheeks, and for the first time in a very, very long time she held a live baby.

Behind her she hears Sam calling a pediatrician and thinks, "Do we even have a pediatrician anymore?"

The baby cries and she looks at Axel, "Where's your wife?"

Norm answers loudly over the baby's cries, "You're holding her."

# Chapter 6



She felt the book in her purse. She had bought it on her way home yesterday. That seemed like such a long time ago now. It was a bit of money but she didn't care and it was quite a find, being paper and all. What a night. She never would have believed it could happen in her wildest dreams.

How would she tell Aaron. A live baby. Norm Fuckin' Bricker with a live baby. She was happy, scared, alive, hopeful and confused.

Yesterday she had hoped the book would bring her back to a simpler time that did not feel simple when it was happening, but simpler in retrospect for sure. She was tired of all the death. Death on the wrong end of the timeline. It's not how it was supposed to be. She wanted to go back to when she saw the looks on their faces. The sheer joy and wonder at the miracle that was placed at the chests of sweaty moms. She wanted to go back to dads passing out and moms and nurses looking at one another chuckling. She wanted midwifes and doctors working together to help fulfill dreams. She wanted to watch the miracle of the spiritualist and the mother working together to create a human being.

So she bought a book, a real book!

But no book could bring that back now. With her hand on the door she thinks back to when they were both in college at

Johns Hopkins and studying medicine. Aaron was convinced Alzheimer's Disease was linked to a virus that sits dormant in one's brain until a person ages.

While groundbreaking research pointed to protein oligomers as the cause of AD, Aaron did not agree. "The death of nerve cells and tissue loss is caused by oligomers gone rogue but why!!! They are all wrong about the why." he would rant as Mary tried to calm him down. "It is all about the prions and we need to be studying CWD in deer before it jumps to US!!"

The Center for Infectious Diseases had been studying Chronic Wasting Disease in animals, especially deer, for years and were recently concerned about a possible jump to humans. "Of course they think it will be spread by meat eating. They are so primal. But no one is looking at how the cow got the disease to start with and what if we could all be exposed just by hiking in the woods or something. I mean look at COVID19. NOBODY believed a pandemic could start with a pig, for God sakes, and look what happened there!"

Mary giggled at "how the cow" and tried to turn away before he saw her. But she was too late and off he went on an hour long lecture on how he would prove that we are all exposed at one time or another to CWD and carry it with us and once he shows everyone he is right it will cure all illnesses, including damned Alzheimer's and make death obsolete.

Mary preferred to focus on birth, *her* chosen profession.

She never would have guessed back then that her husband working to save the world from disease and death would lead to a birth being the most lifeless act two humans could experience. Nor could she face that HIS passion led to HER profession, her life's work, her joyful dreams of helping women to bring babies into the worl, being reduced to scraping lifeless uteruses filled with the remains of dead fetuses out of women who routinely gave birth, "just in case" a soul would find THEIR baby.

Well a soul found one baby last night. That baby found her own mom's soul, thanks to Norm.

How did he have the presence of mind to do a C-Section right when that women killed herself and to have the dad be there as a spiritualist to direct the soul, "Holy Cow. I wonder if the mom even knew her husband was one of them," she says, talking to herself as she stares blindly at the front door of their home thinking of the Medical Journals from back in the day showing happy moms and dads holding their infants, their LIVE infants.

Aaron would think she was a fool to believe in the old ways. She could hear him yelling, "It's just not scientific," as they fought about things she had witnessed in deliveries. If anyone could have convinced him it would have been Elaine Bricker. After all she gave her life, her soul for her granddaughter.

He was so pensive during those days. She knew he was with someone else around that time and thought he just wasn't that into her. He was wrapped up in his studies and his research and she thought he just didn't have time for her. Then one day right after Elaine died he asked her to marry him. She wondered if she should say yes given his science based attitude about life and insisting souls didn't exist and stories she told him were just her imagination.

"Well, he wasn't there," she thought. "He was off saving the world from death and creating a living hell."

But she said yes anyway, thinking Elaine's death had changed him. They both lost Norm to the trial and all of that craziness and they were so busy finishing thier studies they just didn't have time.

The door opens with her hand firmly clutching the knob and she is almost knocked down the stairs by her husband as he blows past her. "Aaron, wait I have something to tell you."

Running to the car he yells as he struggles to get the door open and his coat on all at the same time, "Mary, it will have to wait. A live baby has been BORN!"

# Chapter 7

*Janine Eelie Bricker*

He never came around anymore. At the beginning he would come by with the baby. Her sweet baby. How could she ever forgive him? It was his fault she lost everything. First her mother, then her mind, then her baby and eventually her dad. He was broken. Who could blame him after all he went through? Just looking at her had to remind him of it ALL; her death, the trial, the publicity and ridicule, and picketing. How could people who believed in a God of love judge another human being so harshly?

How could they be filled with so much hate for someone with a different belief system that they allow the government to take all he has left as a punishment for the gift of life.

It was a choice, a gift, her mother gave to her. It was none of their business if one valued the life of a child, of a baby, of the future, over one's own life. It was none of their business to take all he had worked so hard for as punishment for an act of love.

Knowing her mom, she would have done it a thousand times despite any punishment. Knowing her dad he would have fought for Elaine's right to choose until the day he died. But he will never die now. Aaron took that choice away 25 years ago. Everything was lost because he couldn't let life just be.

She is sitting in a room with bright lights, the kind that buzz. "It is always so bright here," she thinks. "One can never see the beams or the dancers."

She turns from the window and searches the room for a friendly face. Visiting hours were always the worst. Terry's mother came everyday with smiles and kisses. Terry just stared into space, belted into her wheelchair by the aid and covered by a blanket so Terry's mother could pretend that Terry was normal and didn't have to be tied down. Terry's mother told funny stories to Terry and pet her hair. But Terry's mother did not give up her soul for her grandchild that slipped lifelessly out of Terry, sending Terry into a hysteria that only drugs and a belted wheelchair could fix. Terry will never forgive her mother for being so selfish and has told Janine every time she hides her meds in her cheek and spits them out when the aid isn't looking, that she would, "Kill that selfish Bitch." if she ever got out of here.

Janine knows how lucky she is to have her daughter all because of her mother's beautiful gift to her. But the trial and the ridicule was too much for her. She wishes she had the strength to endure all of it, like her dad. She wishes she lived with her daughter in an apartment on the west side, one of the ones with a million different ethnicities all dwelling in stacked boxes sharing smells and noises. It's a place where beams of light would shine through her window when the sun was setting and she would watch the soul dancers and then it would be dark. "It's never dark there." she thinks. "I wish it could be dark."

She wishes things didn't happen as they did and that she didn't let Aaron talk her into giving her up. She felt so guilty. Guilty for being pregnant. Guilty for having the baby. Guilty for her mom's death. Guilty for going crazy. Guilty for ruining everyone's life. If she hadn't felt so guilty she would be living in an apartment and would have raised her daughter and who knows if Jessie would be married by now and be living next to her on the East side with HER family watching souls dance in the sunlight.

The news is on the television and the aids and the nurses and Terry's mom and the old man with the grey curly hair who thinks he is a woman are all watching the news. Janine turns away thinking how Terry will have a chance to talk later if the aids aren't paying attention to everyone's meds. She starts walking down the bright hall to go to her room, the nurse behind the glass looks up, a little pissed that she is doing paperwork while everyone else is watching the TV, and smiles. Janine starts to smile back but is stopped by a sound. A sound so unreal that she barely remembers what it is. The nurse looks at her, expecting Janine to be making the sound, but she is not. They both look at the TV screen and when Terry's mom drops into a chair like she fainted they see it, her, him, a baby. They hear the cry and Janine's stomach turns upside down and she vomits all over the nurse as she leaves her glass house. "I want my baby, " she sobs. But the nurse ignores her and rushes toward the TV leaving Janine to collapse into her own vomit.

The phone rings and Norm can barely remember what to do. It has been a LONG fucking night and the last thing he wants to do is relive the story to some reporter that he used to supervise before the lawsuit so they can get the lead story in today's *Record Herold*. It's all digital now and he misses the days when you went deaf from the presses and always had black ink on your hands.

Why does all this shit happen to HIM!

The phone continues to ring. He chose the old fashioned ring tone that sounded like the phones that hung on the wall in his youth, nostalgia he guesses, as he takes a long drink of his Bourbon, one of the only bonuses of his fateful history. Some fan leaves him a bottle every year on the anniversary of Elaine's death, his granddaughter Jessie's birthday.

Janine...he stares at the phone and slowly gets up from his chair to answer and stop the ringing. He looks at the number and doesn't recognize it but for some reason decides to answer. Maybe he just needs to hear another human, "Hello, if this is a reporter, no comment."

He starts to hang up and hears, "Mr. Bricker, Mr. Bricker... please. Mr. Bricker."

He looks at the number again and says, "What has happened to Janine?"

# Chapter 8

*Janine and Norm*


He walks into the cold metal building, through the cold metal doors and thinks, "You need Goddamned sunglasses in here."


He stops at the security counter which reminds him of the rows of bank tellers back in the day, showing his ID to the woman at the desk who looks at him with pity in her eyes. He hates pity which is why he has tried to be anonymous the last many years.

It was all too much. It is still too much. Yet here he is, thrust into the light again, quite literally here at the hospital, no wait, the *Community for the Mentally Challenged*, and figuratively with the reporters and government all over him last night because of the birth. He falters in his thoughts as the woman hands him his ID and instructs him to the sixth floor. "I am so sorry to hear about your daughter." she says.

"There is nothing to be sorry about." he says and walks away.

The elevevator doors open to an all too familiar smell. A cross between rubbing alchohol and bleach that some find pleasant and clean and Norm finds, well, repulsive. He walks to the waiting room where he has sat for far too many hours in his past. The TV is on but he intentionally chooses a chair with his back to the screen. There is no one else in the area and it seems as if they are on lockdown or some such thing. He recalls how these visits used to tear up his soul so he stopped coming after a while. He hears the secretary say, "He will see you now."

"While the incident was completely against protocol and we want you to know the nurse has been reprimanded to the highest degree, the circumstances that caused her to abandon her station were highly irregular, one might even say a once in a lifetime event."

"Tell me about it." Norm says under his breath.

"And because of those circumstances we have not fired Nurse Smith. Because of the quick actions of the orderly your daughter will have a full recovery."

"Well the orderly should get a raise if you ask me and despite the 'circumstances,' your nurse left the door to the station open and unattended allowing my daughter, a patient here for the last 20 some years,  to enter and ingest copious amounts of dangerous, one might even say deadly, drugs in an attempt to kill herself. Is that about right?"

"Well, of course we are very aware of Janine's triggers and the nurse, well Janine vomited on her and the baby was crying on the TV. But one must understand that the birth of a live baby...a LIVE baby is such a rare thing it distracted everyone and while we are partially responsible,"

"Partially responsible, huh?"

"Well, yes sir, I mean Janine did take the meds herself, no one forced them down her throat."

"We are done here," Norm said standing, clenching his fists, trying hard not to clock this guy like back in his boxing days. "Bring me to my daughter."

She wasn't tied down or drugged which made him relieved.

You never know what you are going to walk into at the Community for the Mentally Challenged. Her hair was just like her mother's, it glowed in the fluorescent light. He allowed himself a moment he rarely could afford and remembered Elaine holding Janinne that first day; the day when he saw her so sad in the room with the light on her belly and the pain on her face that originated partly from in her pelvis and partly in the deepest part of her soul; the day the protesters almost caused her to give birth in the car and the day they watched this part of them, this baby,  take her first breath, inhaling her grandmother's soul, so graciously given, from a natural death to a natural birth.

"Dad, it is so nice to see you."

So maybe not drugged UP but definitely drugged.

"Me too, little girl."

He hesitantly walked over to her. He hadn't been there to

visit in quite a while. It had become too much to bare. But she

hugged him. It was a long, loving hug and whispered in his ear, "I

heard her cry. She is one of ours."

He held her tear streaked face in his hands and kissed her

forehead and turned around to leave. "Why did I come?" he said to

himself. "It never changes."

"Dad, I am not crazy. Not this time," a soft smile kissed her

lips. "Her cry is one of ours. One of our souls."

He turns to her. "How do you know? How could you know?

There is no one but us, you and me, left."

He tried not to sound angry. She was so very broken by no

fault of her own. In fact, if he was honest, it was all HIS fault

and maybe that was why he couldn't bring himself to visit her,

creating distractions upon distractions until months turned into

years of no contact. Yes, that was it, guilt. He introduced them. He didn't listen closely to Elaine. She told him but he was too busy with his career and covering all the breaking news. He didn't suspect a thing.

"There is no one but us." he said again.

"But you're wrong. We just don't know where he sent her, where she went. She could be right next to us and we wouldn't know. What if she married? What if she got pregnant? What if a soul we didn't *know* was one of ours, saw her pain, my daughter's pain at losing baby after baby and waited for the right moment, the moment of breath and gave her child life. My daughter and my *grand*daughter are alive."

He stared at her in disbelief. Someone had been talking to her. Someone let the reporters talk to her. How could she know what he had done. She was crazy to think the soul was theirs but he felt it too as he cradled the baby in his arms. That soul had stirred a love, a hope, he had not let himself feel for many years, too many years. But feeling that connection was beyond his control the moment she cried. Why had he felt for that girl, that neighbor for so long? Why did her crying when she lost her babies bother him so much when so many mothers' cries had pierced his doors and walls daily and he felt nothing? But if Janine was right then that meant...

He had to get out of this place. He suddenly felt panicked and hot, like the walls were closing in. "I have to go baby. I have to go."

He kissed her cheek. He had to get out of this place! He had to get *her* out of this place. They were cruel. They didn't understand. Community my ass! This wasn't a community!

He had to talk to Aaron, that asshole.

"I have to leave, sweetheart. I have to think. But I will be back and we will get you out of here, I promise.”

She saw the sweat on his brow and the look of sheer panic. She had seen it before when the police came to the door back then. “Oh daddy, don’t worry. Think of Gran Dusanka and Gran Eelie and all of the traditions they taught mom and mom taught me and I would have taught…,” she stops.

“Taught Jessie.” he finishes.

“Yes, taught Jessie. We need to start saying her name more. I feel like she is very close to us.”

“She may be closer that you think." he says over his shoulder as he walks out the door. "I will be back with a court order, so start packing.”

He said this with a smile of fake assurance because there is no way he could get her released without Aaron’s influence.

Maybe time had mellowed his ego. Just maybe he would see how

he had ruined their lives and take pity.

As he walks past security he says, "Fucking asshole."

The guard replies, "Have a nice day!"

# Chapter 9

*Norm*

"I killed OUR Jessie."

He sits in the darkness of his car outside of the Community for the Mentally Challenged, after seeing his daughter, after seeing the hope in her eyes, after hearing her say, "MY daughter and MY granddaughter" and sobs.

# Chapter 10

*Aaron and Janine*

The trip to the hospital seemed to take hours. A live birth, incredible. No one had died. He searched the records before he left. He was on live notification from every hospital in the country so he could be in on the autopsy before the government got there and fucked it all up just so they could prove some poor slob had offed themselves to have a grandkid and arrest the family.

He flashes back to a moment in time he would like to forget.

Janine's face flashes before him like a ghost. He told her to abort the baby and not tell her parents. He had her all set on it. But the damned Right to Lifers picketing the Planned Parenthood, the same group that haunts him today trying to keep people from ending it all, talked, no, shamed her out of it and so they had to tell Norm and Elaine.

He let the punch hit him. He could have ducked or moved or something but he deserved it. Why the hell didn't Janine just end it.

Another punch caught him squarely in the jaw reminding him that Norm used to box.

Elaine tried to tell him about these souls, begging him to stop his research, "The body is just a body," she said, "it is not a person until it breathes in its soul with its first breath. Stopping death is unnatural."

THAT is not scientifically sound and he just dismissed it like he dismissed the idea of a God. As he ducked the third punch, he said, "She should have just gotten rid of it."

"WHAT?? What the FUCK did you just say, you mother fucker," Norm was sweating and out of control.

"Technically daughter fucker but … some things are best left unsaid."

"Aaron!" Elaine screamed.

"Daddy! Stop!"

But there was no stopping him. His best friend had fucked his daughter and gotten her pregnant. Elaine looked exhausted and walked into the house, slamming the door just as Aaron got ahold of Norm and held him in a bear hug until he calmed a little.

BEEEEEEEEEPPPPP!!! "God damn it." he says as he swerves out of the way of an oncoming car. "This traffic sucks. I need to get to that baby. I can't believe I was so wrong. I have to fix it. I was such an ass."

But he can't stop thinking about that day, that circumstance, the genuine gift of love.

"Elaine," he thought. How he admired her and what she had done for Janine and their Jessie. He remembered how beautiful she smelled, like water.

Elaine died the day Jessie was born. For Norm it was dejavu. Aaron remembers Norm and Elaine telling him about the whole Eelie dying thing when Janine was born and the souls being a part of the family and thinking Norm was full of shit.

But when Jessie was born after Elaine's death it was something he HAD to think seriously about for the first time.

The baby smelled like...water. And the smile on Janine's face as she held her for the first time was the most beautiful thing he had ever seen. Her cry was the most beautiful thing he had ever heard.

But the darkness descended almost immediately after that. Postpartum they all said, but he knew it was the sorrow and survivor's guilt that engulfed her every time she looked at Jessie and thought of her mother's sacrifice and the hell the government was putting her father through.

He had set Janine and Jessie up in an apartment near his work but not so close that Mary would ever find out. He was serious about Mary. She was his future. Janine was a little lapse in judgement and a lot too much tequila. But Janine and Jessie had everything they could ever want or need and all was pretty good for awhile.

Then Mary's friend, "What was her name?" he thought as he sat in traffic ready to explode. Why was he thinking about all of this NOW?

He couldn't remember her name but she had a girl about the same time and named her Terry. "Must have been one of the last souls available." he thinks just as the traffic starts to move.

"Everything would have been fine if that bitch wasn't such a Right to Lifer, sicking those assholes on poor ole Norm like that; him having to go to court and losing everything all because Elaine gave up her soul for her granddaughter. That drove Janine right over the edge. And what was I supposed to do. I couldn't raise Jessie. It would have ruined everything. But I never should have just left her like that."

He parks and gets himself together. He was at the hospital, pushing through the reporters and TV cameras with his head down and security guards escorting him in. " In the end Norm lost his wife, his daughter, his granddaughter and everything he worked for all because of ..."

A baby cries.

# Chapter 11



*Axel Truman and Mylove Jessie*

He slept all night in the hosptial while doctors tried to poke and prod and investigate his daughter. He had to be on guard for her life and for Jessie's death. "What would happen to he and the baby? He would have to lie and say the C-Section is what killed Jessie." he thought as he held his daughter's, his wife's, sweet hand as she slept.

"What a world you've been born into, my love."

He always called Jessie that and now, after seeing what he saw last night, that would be the name he called his daughter for they were one and the same, she and Jessie. His mom trained him as a spiritualist just about the time all the souls dried up. But no one knew how that would manifest itself at the time. So when he heard the cry and looked into the kitchen to see Jessie not there, he knew what she had done. She just couldn't take another one, dead, and he ran to her but...

She was so alone her whole life after her parents abandoned her. He father was some famous guy, he knew that, but she never spoke of her mom. They grew up together. He was drawn to her as far back as he could remember and as they got older there was no mistaking the fact that they belonged together. His mother said it was a sin. That they were siblings. But only in name. And that kind of love only happens to very special people. Knowing you love someone from the moment your souls touch is a gift. So they got married. But with no support from anyone they had to live in the apartments. He looks at their daughter, who owns that soul he fell in love with and cries.

There is nothing he can do now. There isn't much the government can take away anyway. They were poor.  What happened. It is all a blur. There was no knock. He just came in. How did he know what was happening? He acted like he lived there. He acted like he knew she was pregnant and knew who they were and knew she was going to take her life.

"Who was that guy and how the hell did he know how to do that?" he said outloud as he turned from his daughter.

"That's what I want to know."

Axel turned to see Mary Mathews' husband standing behind him. He had heard he was some famous scientist and expected he would be wanting to examine his daughter or interrogate him. "Not interested in making any statements, sir."

"Oh, I know what you're thinking. You think I am here on behalf of the government but THAT couldn't be farther from the truth."

"Well, I am sure Mary told you all about last night and if you think I am ratting out that old man you are mistaken."

"Wait, Mary?"

"Yup, she knew the guy and acted like they were old friends. And I don't know if Jessie took her own life or if he killed her when he cut the baby out of her belly but either way I will …" his tears flowed out of him without a sound.

All of the hopes and dreams of a live child were covered in the blood of his wife. An angel was sent to them to save his daughter's life with the knife his wife used to end hers. And Axel knew either he or the stranger or both would have to answer for this.

"No one really cares about death anymore. But life...especially the life of an infant.. well, that brings out the worst in people." He turns and looks Aaron in the eyes, "Thanks to you."

"Why don't we start over," said Aaron. "I am Dr. Aaron Mathews and yes, I cured death several years ago, as you may have read in the paper. One of the unfortunate consequences of my research and the government overreacting, as they are known to do, is that we ran out of souls. I must admit the soul giving life to a human body was beyond my science trained mind at the time but I was wrong and I have promised myself to rectify this grave error in judgement on my part.

"Without souls we do not have live babies. Yet here I stand looking at a live baby. So, I need to hear this story from the beginning. So, before the government gets involved and you end up in jail I would like to help you leave here, with your child so we can figure

this all out. It is apparent you know my wife, who by the way, did

NOT relate any of this story to me this morning as I rushed over

here to meet you.  I think I have  a perfect place for you and your

daughter to kind of 'hide out' until we figure this all out. Are you

in? We don't have a lot of time"


Axel's face softens as the door opens behind Aaron revealing

Mary and says, "Yes, I think that would be a wonderful idea."

# Chapter 12

*Norm*

He wakes to light. It is streaming through his window like a sabor straight into his eyeball, searing his brain like a well done steak.

"Fucking Bourbon."

"Fucking life for that matter."

He moves his head and he looks down to see if his brain spattered on the floor. But no. He's good.

He looks at his phone expecting a call from the government. "What was that pricks name? Garfield or something. What a douche."

That is not something he wants to go back to this morning. He has enough on his plate. He has to call fucking Aaron. Get Janine out of the nut house. Go to the hospital and find his granddaughter.

His granddaughter.

He drops his hands to his lap and stares at the dancers in the beam. What if Janine is right? What if he killed his granddaughter to save his great granddaughter? Would she have died anyway? He thought so. He remembers hearing the scream. That was NOT the scream of a lost baby. He doesn't remember why or how he got up there.

"The cursed thin walls. Why did I even hear her?"

He knocked her husband out of the way and looked down to see all the blood and the knife. He saw the life still in her eyes and she looked at him like she knew him. He rememberslooking at her husband and saying, "I am going to save your baby. Your wife is going to save your baby."

And before he knew it he cut open her uterus with the same knife she slit her wrist with and just as he had seen when Janine was born and when Jessie was born, he saw the wisp of spirit move into the baby's mouth as she took her first breath. But the dad, he was in prayer, like a dancer almost, moving the wisp toward the baby. It couldn't be. It was all too unreal. Was he a spirit guide?

"I am fucking nuts. What a fucking night!"

He grabs his phone and calls Aaron Mathews, that son of a bitch. That is exactly how he entered the number in his directory. Aaron Mathews, that son of a bitch.

He calls and leaves this message, "Aaron, we gotta get her out of that nut house. Meet me at the Community. Oh and by the way, you're still a son of a bitch."

# Chapter 13

*Aaron, Axel, Mary, My Love, Janine, and Norm*

My Love cries and Aaron stares at Axel in panic. They are sneaking down a stairwell used just the night before by Mary to race to the ER and it still smells like cat piss.

OK, This is where your journey begins. Send me your best work at

teenavaughndannibale@outlook.com.

I cannot wait to see where you take my friends.

Good writing,

*Teena*